Windows to the World

Alice Bianchi-Clark
Illustrated by Chloe Chang

He totters under the weight of thick albums.

And he strains his eyes through his magnifying glass.

Looking after stamps is a big responsibility.

Monday to Saturday, Nonno sorts through his gazillion stamps.

But I love Sundays best because there's no sorting to do.

"Aren't these wonderful, Alexander? Come."

"Stamps are windows to the world.
Every stamp has a story to tell."

"Tell me a stamp story, Nonno."

"Which one?"

"You know which one."

I snuggle into Nonno. He clears his throat and begins.

"The world's very first stamp was the Penny Black. It was the first day of May 1840, back when messages were still sent by carrier pigeon or on horseback…"

We leaf through the crinkly pages of his albums.

"These will be yours someday, Alexander. When you have something special, it's good to share," he says, patting me on the shoulder.

I think I know what "someday" means because it makes me feel all wriggly inside. And there's another thing – I don't want to hurt Nonno's feelings but…

what if I don't want to be a collector?

When my schoolteacher mentions the Philatelic Museum, I ask Nonno whether he knows about it.

"Of course. It's the home, the heaven of stamps. It's impossible not to love the quiet dignity of it: the musty smell of printed paper, the gleaming vitrines, the ticking of the temperature gauges on the walls…"

I have no idea what Nonno is talking about.

But when Nonno takes me there, I understand. Inside, it's neither too hot, nor too cold. Stamps are safe and snug behind glass. Friendly guards smile in every room. And here, everyone can enjoy them, not just me.

We even get to meet the curator. And, when she asks about his stamps, Nonno glows.

That's when I have an idea.

Sadly, Nonno doesn't like it.

"Isn't sharing with me and sharing with the world the same thing?" I say, patting his shoulder.

Nonno gathers his albums and hides. I doubt Nonno's teacher ever talked about sharing in school.

"Imagine your precious stamps sitting alongside our museum collection's Penny Black," I read to a closed door.

But Nonno still won't come out.

"When you have something special, it's good to share," I whisper through the keyhole.

Finally, I hear Nonno's slippers shuffle and his door clicks open.

Now that Nonno's stamps have found a home at the Philatelic Museum, Monday to Saturday, Nonno runs guided tours.

He no longer strains his eyes, totters under thick albums, or wobbles on ladders.

But I love Sundays best because that's when he runs tours with me. We delight crowds with the Penny Black story. And after Nonno says, "Stamps are windows to the world…"

I don't miss a beat — "Every stamp has a story to tell."

Charlotte Tebay (1819–1901)
First Female Member of the Philatelic Society London and Philatelist

Sir Daniel Cooper (1821–1902)
(Politician, Philanthropist and Philatelist)

Jean-Baptiste Moens (1833–1908)
(Belgian Stamp Dealer and Philatelist)

Ernest R Ackerman (1863–1931)
(US Congressman and Philatelist)

King George V (1865–1936)
(King of the British Empire and Philatelist)

President Franklin Delano Roosevelt (1882–1945)
(US President and Philatelist)

Charlie Chaplin (1889–1977)
(English Actor, Filmmaker and Philatelist)

Casimiro Cardascia (1944–)
(Mathematician and Philatelist)

Alexander Tybalt Darling (2010–)
(Student and Philatelist)

Now both our names are spelled in golden letters next to the word "Philatelist."

"How am I a philatelist?" I ask.

"A philatelist is someone who looks after stamps."

"Like you?" I ask.

"And you, Alexander," he says, patting my shoulder. "When you have something special…"

I chime in,
"It's good to share."

PARTS OF A STAMP

DESIGN — This is the image on the stamp.

RELATED INSCRIPTION — Sometimes stamps indicate the stamp's theme.

SERRATIONS — The lacelike edges or perforations between stamps and around a stamp.

STAMP FRAME — This is the separation between the design and the serrations.

ISSUING COUNTRY — All stamps must state their country of origin except for Britain.

YEAR OF ISSUE — This is the year a particular stamp was introduced.

FACE VALUE — This is the official selling price of the stamp, stated in its local currency.

IT'S YOUR TURN!

Here's a rare stamp.
Can you identify its parts?

GRONCHI ROSA

This stamp is part of triptych, a set of three stamps, to commemorate Italian President Giovanni Gronchi's state visit to Argentina, Uruguay and Peru in 1961.

Did you know that rare stamps are often the result of printing errors? Compare the contours of Peru with those in an atlas. Do they match?

Does Nonno have this rare pink stamp as well as the correct reprint issued in grey? What about the other two in the series?

Fun facts about the Penny Black,
THE WORLD'S FIRST STAMP

WHY IS IT SO WELL KNOWN?

The Penny Black is the world's first adhesive or self-sticking stamp. It features the profile of Queen Victoria who ruled when the Penny Black was invented. This stamp revolutionised the sending of mail. How? It made it simpler. It allowed for all letters weighing up to 14 grams to be sent anywhere at the flat rate of one penny. This prepayment method proved so popular that writing letters became the new form of communication.

PENNY BLACK, 1840

WHY ITS NICKNAME?

The Penny Black is black in colour and its monetary value is one penny (British currency). This stamp has straight edges and no serrations (lacelike edges). Why? Those had not been invented yet!

WHEN WAS IT FIRST USED?

The Penny Black was issued on the 1st of May 1840. Before 1840, messages were sent by carrier pigeon or on horseback and whoever received the mail paid for its postage on a distance-travelled, per-sheet basis. This made calculating postage complicated.

WHY DOESN'T IT STATE THE COUNTRY OF ORIGIN?

All stamps state where they are from except for British stamps. Why? It's a special privilege awarded to Britain because Britain is where stamps were invented. British stamps always bear a silhouette of the current monarch.

THE PROFILE OF QUEEN ELIZABETH II WAS USED ON BRITISH STAMPS UNTIL HER PASSING IN 2022.

YOUR BEGINNER'S GUIDE TO STAMP COLLECTING

WHAT ARE YOUR INTERESTS?

WHAT ARE YOU PASSIONATE ABOUT?

WHAT TO COLLECT?

You can start building your stamp collection around your interests and what you are passionate about.

WHAT TOOLS MAY BE USEFUL?

MAGNIFYING GLASS — A magnifying glass to examine your stamps in detail.

ALBUMS — Albums for sorting and storage. Ideally, all stamps should be stored somewhere dark and dry to avoid damage due to mould, sunlight and humidity.

WHERE CAN STAMPS BE FOUND?

MAILBOXES

Look through the letters and parcels you receive through the post and check if there are any stamps on them before discarding the envelopes or packages.

FRIENDS & FAMILY

Ask your friends and family to help you collect stamps. This way, you can collect stamps from all over the world. I regularly cut them out of used envelopes and packages I receive in the post, taking extra care not to damage the serrations. I keep them aside for my father in an old biscuit tin.

A Note About This Story

Alice's father, a philatelist, started collecting stamps as a child, after the second world war. He scrimped, swapped and saved for sixty years until his collection spanned several continents and cultures.

When his entire collection was stolen, Alice's son wondered why he hadn't shared it with the world. This innocent comment inspired Alice to write this story.

The Author
Alice Bianchi-Clark is a collector of sorts. Italian by nationality, she has lived and worked in Rome, London, Paris, Beijing and Hong Kong. She currently resides in Singapore with her supportive husband, big-hearted son, menagerie of parrot fish and terrapins, balcony of flowers and library of picture books. Sharing brings her joy.

The Illustrator
As an illustrator based in sunny Singapore, Chloe Chang spends her time reading, drawing and applying sunblock lotion. She graduated from the School of Art, Design and Media (ADM), NTU Singapore, with a degree in Digital Animation. One of her first projects was Mediacorp's 3D-animated children's television series, Lil' Wild, where she was lead character designer. Chloe now focuses on children's book illustration and works with local and International publishers to bring stories to life.

To my father, who taught my son and me that every stamp has a story to tell.
– A.B.

For Arielle, may you look through many windows to many worlds.
– C.C.

The publisher would like to thank the Ministero dello Sviluppo Economico, Italy, for the permission to reproduce the Gronchi Rosa triptych (1961); Crociera Transatlantica triptych (1993) and Pinocchio (1954); and Filatelia delle Poste Vaticane for the permission to reproduce the series of the Cappella Sistina restaurata (1994) in this book.

Windows to the World
ISBN 978 981 5044 17 1

© 2023 Marshall Cavendish International (Asia) Pte Ltd
Text ©2023 Alice Bianchi-Clark
Illustrations © 2023 Chloe Chang

Published by Marshall Cavendish Children
An imprint of Marshall Cavendish International

All rights reserved

No part of this publication may be reproduced, stored in a retrieval system or transmitted, in any form or by any means, electronic, mechanical, photocopying, recording or otherwise, without the prior permission of the copyright owner. Requests for permission should be addressed to the Publisher, Marshall Cavendish International (Asia) Private Limited, 1 New Industrial Road, Singapore 536196. Tel: (65) 6213 9300
E-mail: genref@sg.marshallcavendish.com
Website: www.marshallcavendish.com

The publisher makes no representation or warranties with respect to the contents of this book, and specifically disclaims any implied warranties or merchantability or fitness for any particular purpose, and shall in no event be liable for any loss of profit or any other commercial damage, including but not limited to special, incidental, consequential, or other damages.

Other Marshall Cavendish Offices:
Marshall Cavendish Corporation, 800 Westchester Ave, Suite N-641, Rye Brook, NY 10573, USA • Marshall Cavendish International (Thailand) Co Ltd, 253 Asoke, 16th Floor, Sukhumvit 21 Road, Klongtoey Nua, Wattana, Bangkok 10110, Thailand • Marshall Cavendish (Malaysia) Sdn Bhd, Times Subang, Lot 46, Subang Hi-Tech Industrial Park, Batu Tiga, 40000 Shah Alam, Selangor Darul Ehsan, Malaysia.

Marshall Cavendish is a registered trademark of Times Publishing Limited

Printed in Singapore